THE NEW

Bobbsey
Twins™

#8
THE SECRET
OF THE STOLEN
PUPPIES

LAURA LEE HOPE
ILLUSTRATED BY PAUL JENNIS

A MINSTREL® BOOK

PUBLISHED BY POCKET BOOKS

New York   London   Toronto   Sydney   Tokyo

A MINSTREL PAPERBACK *ORIGINAL*

A Minstrel Book published by
POCKET BOOKS, a division of Simon & Schuster Inc.
1230 Avenue of the Americas, New York, N.Y. 10020

ISBN: 0-671-62659-0

First Minstrel Books printing October, 1988

10 9 8 7 6 5 4 3 2 1

Contents

THE SECRET OF THE STOLEN PUPPIES

1
A Win and a Loss

"Mom, we have something *very* important to tell you," said Flossie Bobbsey. She placed a steaming mug in front of her mother.

"Thank you, Flossie," said Mrs. Bobbsey. "A cup of tea is just what I need right now. Only a few more calls to make and then I'll be through."

"And then you'll come out back so we can tell you something?" asked Flossie.

"I promise," said Mrs. Bobbsey. She dialed the telephone. "Hello, Louise? Well, how's the Lockhart family today? That was such a lovely party you gave last week. And wasn't it a pity that afterward . . ."

Flossie went out to the back porch of the Bobbsey house. Her twin brother, Freddie, and her older sister, Nan, were already there.

Nan was fluffing up an old sofa pillow. She carefully placed it in the corner, next to the wood box.

"That ought to make a good bed for the new puppy," she said. She gave the pillow a punch.

"*If* they let us keep it," groaned Freddie. "You know what Mom and Dad always say— 'Who's going to end up taking care of it?' "

"We just have to convince them that we're really serious about it," said Nan. "*And* that we'll take full responsibility."

"You sound just like Dad," said Freddie.

"When is Bert going to pick it up at the firehouse? When's he going to get here with our puppy?" asked Flossie.

Bert Bobbsey was Nan's twin brother. He and Nan were twelve years old, with brown hair and brown eyes. Flossie and Freddie, the younger twins, were blond and had blue eyes.

"He should be here pretty soon now," said Freddie. "He was going over to the firehouse right after summer softball tryout."

"Chief Johnson said people are coming to pick out puppies this week," said Flossie. "I guess Sparkle, their mother, will be glad to have her room back to herself."

"It must have been pretty crowded in there with seven puppies," said Freddie. "I hope Bert picks out the best one."

"We ought to put some newspapers in that

corner," said Nan. "Better not take chances till the puppy's trained. Floss, see if Mom is still on the phone."

Flossie went back inside. She poked open the door leading to the hall and listened. Her mother was still on the phone.

"Yes, that's right, Friday night. And we're hoping you can come. It's the first time we're using those new caterers, the Milligans. They did the Lockharts' party last week. And they catered the Porters' anniversary dinner. Everyone just raves about them."

Flossie sighed. The big party was the most important thing on Mrs. Bobbsey's mind right now.

Flossie went back outside.

"Still talking," she reported.

"Well, that gives us time to go over our plan," Nan said. "First we show her what a nice place we've made for the puppy."

"Then I tell her about keeping track of chores on my computer," said Freddie. He unfolded a printout showing a timetable with everyone's chores. "Feeding. Walking. Cleaning."

"What do I do?" asked Flossie.

"You wait for Dad and launch the attack on him." Nan's eyes twinkled. "And Bert gives him the old 'man's best friend' routine."

"Dad's not going to be easy," said Freddie. "He keeps saying we won't take care of a dog.

Remember last week when the Lockharts' puppy disappeared? Right after their party? Dad said they were careless."

"Mom said they should have kept the dog on a leash," said Nan.

"Mom just puts on an act," said Freddie, "but she really likes dogs. Every time she gets a free dog-food sample in the supermarket, she gives it away. Sometimes she even gives it to old man Gower to feed to his stray dogs."

"I don't like the way Mr. Gower looks," said Flossie.

"Just because he's kind of rumpled looking and never shaves doesn't mean he's a bad guy," said Nan, looking around the porch.

"I bet he has more dogs than anyone else in Lakeport," Freddie added.

"Speaking of food, why don't we get a bowl of puppy chow ready?" Nan suggested.

"I'll go get it," said Freddie.

"And I'll fill up a bowl with water," said Nan.

"I'll watch for Bert," offered Flossie.

She poked her head inside the kitchen door as the others went off on their errands. Mrs. Bobbsey was still on the phone.

"I know," she was saying into the receiver. "We weren't planning to give such a fancy party. But the Milligans came to us and offered their services—at a price we just couldn't turn down. They should be coming by any time now with some menus. What? Oh yes, we're going to ask Alice Porter. She's so upset about her loss. That's the second one I've heard about."

Flossie took an apple from the fruit bowl on the table and went out back.

Maybe I'll just start walking toward the firehouse, she thought. That way I'll see Bert and the puppy first.

Flossie started to skip down the driveway. She almost bumped into a woman who was walking toward her.

"Whoops!" said Flossie.

The woman was tall and carried a large blue envelope. At her side was a much shorter man with a neatly trimmed mustache.

"Oh!" said the startled woman. "We're looking for the Bobbsey residence."

"This is it," said Flossie. She looked at the two people curiously. "I'm Flossie Bobbsey."

"Isn't that nice." The woman smiled at Flossie. "I'm Vera Milligan. This is my husband, Albert. We're here to see your mother."

Nan and Freddie came around the side of the house.

"This is my sister, Nan, and my twin brother, Freddie," said Flossie. She introduced the Milligans.

"It's so nice to see there are three of you

children. We like to have young people around. They're such a help," said Mrs. Milligan.

"Actually, there are four of us, counting my brother Bert," Nan explained. "We might as well go in the back way since we're almost there anyhow."

"Oh, you have a dog," said Mrs. Milligan, looking at the pillow on the porch. "How nice."

"Not yet, but we hope we're getting one today," Flossie blurted out.

"That's a secret, Flossie!" cried Freddie.

"Then maybe you shouldn't tell us," said Mrs. Milligan.

"Bert is going to pick it up at the fire station this afternoon," Flossie went on. "I hope he gets the right one. There are seven of them. And they all look just like their mother, white with black spots. They're dalmatians."

"But we're just about to tell Mom now—and Dad later," said Nan. "So we'd appreciate . . ."

"Your secret is safe with us," said Mrs. Milligan.

"But we don't want to ruin your surprise. Maybe we should come back later," said Mr. Milligan.

"Albert, we have an appointment," said Mrs. Milligan firmly.

Mrs. Bobbsey called from inside the house.

"Now, what is so important that Flossie

made me a cup of tea? Or that Freddie offered to vacuum the front hallway?"

"There's something we want to tell you, Mom," said Freddie. "Can you come out back?"

"Oh, Mr. and Mrs. Milligan, there you are," said Mrs. Bobbsey. She stepped out onto the porch. "I see you've met Nan and Freddie and Flossie. Won't you come in?"

"I know we were going to talk about menus," said Mr. Milligan. "But the more I think about it, the more I feel you should have a chance to go over them on your own first." He took the big blue envelope from his wife and handed it to Mrs. Bobbsey.

"Are they that complicated?" asked Mrs. Bobbsey, frowning.

"No, but it would really make things easier for you. In fact, why don't you just pick a few things? You can let us know what you have in mind. Then we can talk about it later," said Mr. Milligan. "Let's go, Vera. The car's out front."

Mrs. Milligan seemed a little annoyed, but she quickly followed her husband down the driveway.

"I suppose they're right," Mrs. Bobbsey said. "I should look these over. But it really won't matter what I pick. I know their cooking is wonderful. And their prices couldn't be lower."

"Uh . . . Mom . . . if you could forget about the party for a minute . . ." said Nan.

"We have a secret. At least, sort of. Maybe," said Flossie.

"I hope it has nothing to do with that old pillow over there and those— Oh no, wait a minute. Don't tell me," said Mrs. Bobbsey. "You've taken one of Mr. Gower's strays and brought it here!"

"No!" cried Flossie. "It's a puppy!"

"A dalmatian puppy from the firehouse," Freddie added quickly.

"We all promise to take care of it. Freddie has all the chores on his computer already," said Nan.

"Bert's bringing it home," said Flossie. "Please, Mom, please!"

"Okay. All right. For the time being," said Mrs. Bobbsey. "I'll say yes . . ."

"I hear a *but* coming," said Nan.

"You're right," said Mrs. Bobbsey. "Your father and I will have to discuss it. And, if we agree, you can keep it. But no final decision until he gets home. Is that understood?"

The three young Bobbseys nodded their heads.

"Now I'm just going to look over these menus," said Mrs. Bobbsey. She went back into the house.

Time passed slowly that afternoon.

"It's taking Bert forever," said Freddie. He was tightening the bolts on his bicycle for the fifth time.

"Dad will probably be home before Bert gets here with the puppy," Flossie said glumly. She reached over and fluffed up the pillow on the porch floor.

"There he is!" shouted Nan, looking down the driveway.

Bert Bobbsey marched up the walk. But he was empty-handed.

"Where is it?" asked Flossie.

"Yeah, Bert, where's the puppy?" asked Freddie.

"There isn't any puppy," Bert said angrily. "It's gone."

"Someone else took our puppy?" asked Nan. "Did Chief Johnson make a mistake, or—"

"There's no mistake," said Bert. "Our puppy is gone. And so are all the others."

"What happened to them?" asked Flossie.

"They've been stolen," said Bert. "Every one of those puppies has been stolen!"

2

Where There's Smoke . . .

"Stolen!" screamed Flossie.

Mrs. Bobbsey heard the cry and rushed outside.

"What happened?" she asked.

Bert explained the situation.

"I got to the firehouse sort of late. There were a lot of guys trying out for the summer softball team."

"Did you make the team?" asked Freddie.

"Sure." Bert smiled.

"What about the puppy?" insisted Flossie.

"I'm coming to that," said Bert. "I got to the firehouse and went to the room in back, but it was empty. So I went to the office and asked Chief Johnson where all the puppies were."

"People were supposed to get them this week," said Nan. "Maybe they came early."

"No way," said Bert. "I was the first one there. The chief told me that the puppies had disappeared. All of them. The only thing he could figure was that they'd been stolen."

"What about poor Sparkle?" asked Flossie.

Bert could tell that his little sister was very upset. "She's okay. She was having her supper in the chief's office while I was there."

"This is very strange," said Mrs. Bobbsey. "Who would take seven dalmatian puppies, anyhow?"

"Maybe someone like old man Gower," said Freddie.

"Nah," said Bert. "He just picks up lost or stray dogs. Then he takes them home and feeds them. He even finds their owners, or he finds them new homes."

"Maybe he's changed," insisted Freddie.

"Mr. Gower is strange, but he wouldn't steal," said Mrs. Bobbsey. "But this isn't the first I've heard about missing puppies."

"The Lockharts!" said Flossie.

"That's right," said Mrs. Bobbsey. "Their new cocker spaniel disappeared right after their party last week. And the Porters just told me that they've lost their new little beagle."

"Sounds like someone's trying to grab every puppy in Lakeport," said Bert angrily.

"Including ours." Nan sighed.

"I hope whoever took it is feeding him his puppy chow," said Freddie.

"Well, I'd better look into feeding a bunch of party guests this Friday," said Mrs. Bobbsey. "Let's let the police take care of the missing puppies."

She went back inside the house.

"I'll just bet missing puppies is real high on the list at the police station," said Bert.

"Maybe we ought to go over to the firehouse to take a look around," said Freddie.

"Good idea," said Nan.

"Go ahead. I have something to do first," said Bert.

"Let's go," said Flossie. "Right *now.*"

Bert ran into the house. The other twins headed for the firehouse.

As they stepped inside, Sparkle looked up at them. Then she lowered her tail and slinked off.

"She probably misses her pups," said Nan.

Flossie and Freddie immediately ran to the back of the firehouse, where there was a little storeroom. It wasn't much more than a closet. This was where the puppies had been kept. Now it was empty.

Nan went into the small office on the side of the firehouse. Chief Johnson was seated at his desk, going through some papers.

"Hello, Nan," he said. He crumpled up a

bunch of blue sheets and tossed them into his wastebasket. "Sorry about your puppy. Too bad about all of them, actually. There are going to be some disappointed kids in Lakeport."

"What happened?" asked Nan. "When did they disappear? Didn't anyone see anything?"

"The puppies," said Chief Johnson, "have been gone for only a few hours. And none of us saw a thing."

"Maybe there's a mistake," said Nan hopefully. "Maybe someone wanted to deliver them to their new owners."

"I'm afraid not," said the chief. "None of the puppies had been selected yet. Today was supposed to be the first day for that."

"Then it looks like they really were stolen," Nan said.

"I'm afraid so," said the chief.

Nan felt both very sad and very angry. How could anyone steal puppies? How could anyone be so mean?

Meanwhile, Freddie and Flossie had looked over the entire storeroom. Nothing was missing. Everything looked exactly the way it had when the puppies were there.

"I'm going to get Nan," said Flossie. "Maybe she found out something."

Freddie wandered aimlessly about. He gave one of the fire engine tires a gentle kick. He ran his finger along the shiny red fender.

"They sure keep this place clean," he murmured. He looked around the firehouse. There wasn't a piece of scrap anywhere.

Then Freddie saw a blue paper on the floor. It was round and had holes in it. Freddie thought it looked like the kind of paper his mother put on the plate under the fruit bowl. Maybe it had been under Sparkle's water bowl.

He threw the paper in a wastebasket.

Nan and Flossie walked over to him.

"Any luck? Any clues?" asked Freddie.

"Not really," said Nan.

"The chief is busy planning the Firemen's Ball. He couldn't talk to us any more," said Flossie.

"We might as well— Hey, wait a minute," Freddie said with excitement. "Look over there."

Through the open firehouse doors, they could see two boys outside. One had dark hair and was a classmate of Bert and Nan's, but not a friend.

"Danny Rugg!" said Nan. She walked over to him, followed by Freddie and Flossie.

"We should have known you'd be around," said Freddie. "Anywhere there's trouble . . ."

"Hey, you want trouble? I'll give it to you," said Danny, doubling his fists.

"Looking to go a few rounds, Danny?" said a voice behind him.

Bert Bobbsey got off his bike.

"Who's your friend, Danny?" asked
She looked at the tall, skinny boy standing
to him. The boy peered down at her thr
thick, horn-rimmed glasses.

"I guess you Bobbseys *don't* know e
thing," Danny said with a sneer.
Jamesons moved to Maplewood Avenue
week. Right near my house. And you still
know it."

"I'm Ronald Jameson," said the tall
"Who are you?"

"I'm Nan Bobbsey. This is my brother
my other brother, Freddie, and my
Flossie."

"Oh, the famous Bobbsey twins. Lak
own little super sleuths," said Ronald. H
narrowed as he stared at the twins.

"Yeah, but they're not the only ones
solve crimes," said Danny. "Tell
Ronald."

"Take it easy, Rugg," said the ol
"Let's not waste our valuable time on
detectives."

"Right. We've got things to do. W
to beat you Bobbseys to it," said Da

"What are you talking about?" a
He could see Danny was up to some
that meant trouble.

"The puppies," said Danny. "Me

are going to find them before you or anybody else."

"That's right," said Ronald. He shoved a stick of gum in his mouth. "We'll get the puppies back before you find your first clue."

"Who cares about clues? We just want to save those puppies," Flossie said softly.

"You two really think you know it all," Nan said to Danny and his friend.

"Enough to track down the puppies." Ronald smirked. "Before you do."

"Want to bet?" asked Bert.

"How much?" asked Danny.

"No," said Ronald. "We don't want their money. We're going to beat you Bobbseys. Just for the pleasure of watching you lose."

He nudged Danny, and the two of them walked off down the street.

"What a couple of creeps!" said Nan.

"And Ronald's a real snob," said Flossie.

"We'll show the two of them," said Freddie. "It's just like that mean Danny Rugg to find a ~iend like Ronald."

"Don't worry," said Bert. "We're going to ~nd the puppies first. After you left, I read up ~ missing pets in my Rex Sleuther Handbook, ~d—"

"Oh no," groaned Nan. "Not Rex Sleuther ~ain!"

"Nan, listen," said Bert. "Tell me what you

found out. Then I'll tell you what Rex Sleuther says about it."

While Nan went over her talk with Chief Johnson, Flossie's thoughts wandered. She was beginning to feel a little hungry.

She looked across the street and saw Clover's, her favorite candy store.

"I'll be right back," she said. "I just want to see if Clover's got any CocoLoco candy bars this week."

Inside the candy store, Flossie stared at the chocolates in the long glass case. Behind her was a tall rack. Large bags of potato chips and popcorn and boxes of cookies were stacked on it almost to the ceiling.

For a few minutes, all Flossie could think of was the delicious candy staring her in the face. Then, all of a sudden, there were voices on the other side of the rack. It was Danny Rugg and Ronald Jameson.

Flossie edged up to the rack and listened. She could just make out Ronald's voice.

". . . and all we need is the license," Flossie heard him say.

"Right," said Danny. "And when we get that, we'll be able to fix those Bobbseys for good."

There was something in Danny's voice that sounded meaner than ever. Flossie stepped back quietly. She didn't want them to know she was there.

She started to tiptoe away when a loud voice from the back of the store called:

"Look who's here—Flossie Bobbsey!"

Flossie froze. The store owner's friendly greeting had just announced she was there. She knew that Danny and Ronald must have heard him. And any moment now, they'd be coming after her.

3

Bottles and Boxes

Mr. Clover greeted his favorite customer as he came up the aisle.

"We don't have any CocoLoco bars yet," he said. "How about Mallow Munchees?"

Just then Danny and Ronald came around the corner.

"You little sneak!" shouted Danny. "You were listening, weren't you?"

"I was not," said Flossie. She started to back away toward the door. "Thank you, Mr. Clover, but I was just looking."

"Any time," said Mr. Clover. "How about you boys? Back for seconds so soon?"

Flossie hurried out the door. She ran down the street to tell the others what had happened.

"Want to hear what Danny and Ronald just said?" she asked, half out of breath.

"It boils down to finding a motive," Bert was saying. "That's what the book says. Who would want so many puppies?"

"Danny and Ronald were just talking. I heard them," said Flossie.

"I don't know," said Nan, shaking her head. "Unless they collect dogs, like old man Gower."

"DOESN'T ANYONE WANT TO KNOW WHAT DANNY AND RONALD ALREADY KNOW?" shouted Flossie at the top of her lungs.

"Relax, Floss," said Freddie. "How do you know what they know, anyway?"

"It just so happens," said Flossie, "I heard them talking in the candy store, and Ronald said that all they needed was for Danny to get his license. Then they'd know who stole the puppies."

Bert scratched his head.

"Danny Rugg's too young to get his driver's license," he said. "It doesn't make sense."

"No." Nan sighed. "I agree. You must have missed something, Flossie."

"Okay," said Bert, walking his bike down the street. "Where does that leave us?"

"Well," said Nan, "we talked to Chief

Johnson. Maybe we should talk to some of the people whose puppies have disappeared."

"What about your friend Laura?" asked Flossie.

"Oh, that's right, Laura Johnson. I forgot all about that," said Nan.

"Didn't she get a new Airedale puppy last week?" asked Bert.

"Yes," said Nan, "and it was stolen a few days later. But I didn't even connect that with the others we heard about, the ones Mom just said."

"That's four hits we know about," said Bert. "The dalmatians, the Porters, the Lockharts, and the Johnson puppy."

They had reached the Bobbsey driveway.

"Well, I know what I'm going to do," said Nan. "Tomorrow I'm going over to talk to Laura. That's a start."

The next day, Mrs. Bobbsey caught Nan as she was heading out the front door.

"Nan, did I hear you say you were going somewhere? Would you do me a favor? Could you drop these menus off at the Milligans' shop?"

"Sure," said Nan. "Where is it?"

"On the lake road. Behind that row of warehouses. They do all their work there," Mrs.

Bobbsey said. She stuffed the blue sheets into an envelope. "The address is right here."

Nan looked at the envelope.

"Wow, that's way over on the other side of town," she said. "I know, I'll do some running. Better get into my running clothes."

On her way upstairs, Nan heard the sound of bottles rattling.

"Oh, Freddie," said Mrs. Bobbsey. "These bottles have to go back to the store. You can use the deposit money to buy one of your magazines. We're going to need the space for new empties on Friday."

"Why?" asked Freddie.

"The party, dummy," said Flossie.

Nan heard her mother sigh.

"Flossie, why don't you help him with those bottles? You can split the money."

"Great!" said Flossie.

The Milligan shop was on a small, dark street.

Nan knocked on the door. She waited a long time before Mrs. Milligan opened it.

"Oh, Nan Bobbsey," said Mrs. Milligan, wiping her grease-covered hands on a dirty rag. There was a smudge of soot on her cheek. Nan thought Mrs. Milligan looked as though she'd been fixing a car, not cooking.

"My mother sent this over," said Nan. She handed over the envelope. "She thought you'd want it right away."

"Yes, please come in. Let me just take a look at what she's picked," said Mrs. Milligan.

There was music playing as Nan entered the shop. A fancy tape deck stood on a shelf with a row of cookbooks. On a big table in the center of the room were piles and piles of plates, napkins, doilies, and bright blue party favors.

Looks like blue is their favorite color, thought Nan.

But she didn't see any stoves or sinks.

"Do you cook things here?" she asked. "Or do you have a kitchen somewhere else?"

Mrs. Milligan nodded toward a door on the other side of the room. "We do our cooking in back. Hmmm. These menus look fine. I'll call your mother and tell her myself."

"Then I'll be going," said Nan.

"I'd offer you something," said Mrs. Milligan, "but we're not cooking anything right now. The food processor is broken, and I'm trying to fix it."

I'm glad she wasn't baking cookies with those hands, thought Nan once she was outside.

The short run to Laura's house felt good. Now, if she could just get something, a possible clue, out of Laura.

But her friend wasn't very much help.

"I'm sorry, Nan," said Laura. "I wasn't even home when it happened. My folks were giving a big party—you know, a grown-up thing."

"Mine are doing that this Friday," said Nan.

"All that smiling at everyone. I had to get out of the house," Laura said. "So I went over to Marsha's house, around the corner, to watch TV."

"Where was the puppy? In the yard?" asked Nan.

"No, the garage. We had a sort of pen for it there," Laura said.

"When did it disappear?" asked Nan.

"It was gone when I came home," said Laura. An unhappy expression came over her face. "I'm so miserable. I miss it so much."

Nan gave Laura a friendly hug.

"Do you mind if I take a look out back?" she asked.

"Go ahead," said Laura. "I . . . I'm not going with you. It's too sad. No one's home, so I'm going to visit my aunt. Okay?"

"Fine," said Nan. "I'll just look around for a minute or two."

Nan walked down the driveway to the garage. A huge pile of cartons was stacked up on one side, but the door behind it was open.

She stepped around the stack and peered inside.

The garage looked empty. Clean as a whistle. Nothing but a tattered blanket in the pen.

Suddenly, Nan spotted a crumpled-up piece of paper on the ground.

She picked it up and looked at it. It was a coupon for a twenty-cent discount on Growling Good dog food. It could belong to the Johnsons, thought Nan. Or to a person with a lot of dogs, like Mr. Gower. Nan was determined to find out who had left the coupon in the garage.

She was about to leave when she heard a strange crunching sound. It was like a person walking on gravel.

Nan turned. But before she could see who was coming toward her, the tall stack of cartons came crashing down.

She screamed as she was buried beneath the pile of toppling boxes.

4

A Browsing Surprise

Nan raised her head and saw cracks of daylight around her. She arched her body and found that she could crawl forward with no trouble at all.

Scattering cartons and packing material in all directions, she worked her way up and out.

As she straightened up, she thought she heard the sound of heavy footsteps. Was that someone running down the driveway? Laura? No, the footsteps were too loud.

She looked alongside the garage but didn't see anyone. But as she looked toward the street, an old truck drove by slowly. It was Mr. Gower's. Nan recognized him immediately: his black woolen cap, large nose, and stubbly white beard. His mouth was set in a grim line.

But Nan especially noticed his eyes. They were small, gray—and glaring right at her.

Before she could say or do anything, he was gone.

Nan shivered, then turned back to the garage.

There was quite a mess in front of her. Crepe paper, Styrofoam "popcorn," blue tissue paper, and party streamers had spilled out onto the ground.

That's why the boxes were so light, Nan thought. They're probably leftovers from the party.

Nan decided she'd better clean things up. Then, on the way back, she'd treat herself to a soda. She deserved it!

Meanwhile, Freddie and Flossie had started on their way to the store. Freddie's old red wagon was filled with empty bottles.

"I'll help steer from behind," offered Flossie.

"Just take your turn pulling," said Freddie.

"How much do you think we'll get for all these bottles?" she asked.

"Didn't you count them?" said Freddie. "I know my share exactly. And yours."

"I trust you." Flossie laughed. "But I don't trust Danny Rugg. Or that new kid, Ronald."

"I know what you mean," Freddie said. "We have to find the puppies before they do."

"I just want to pick a puppy and get it home as fast as we can," said Flossie.

"After we do this, I'm going over to the Lockharts'," said Freddie. "Maybe I'll come up with a clue."

"Do you think Nan will find out anything at Laura's house?" asked Flossie.

"I don't know," answered Freddie.

"Well, do you think Bert will find out anything from all those notes he's making about the case?" she asked.

"I don't know," Freddie answered.

"Do you think we'll find the puppies before Danny and Ronald?"

"It's your turn to pull the wagon," said Freddie, trying to change the subject.

"First I'm going to count the bottles," Flossie said. "I want to make sure you added them up right!"

Freddie rolled his eyes.

When they reached the store, Freddie tied the wagon to a lamppost. He and Flossie brought the bottles inside and got their money. Then they headed for the magazine rack.

"I want to see if the new *Hollywood Hotline* has that article on Jessica Jordon in it," Flossie said. "She told me about it in her last letter. You know, she—"

"Looks exactly like you," finished Freddie.

"That's all we hear. Ever since you two got together when those jewels were stolen."

"Everyone says she could be my twin," said Flossie, flipping through the row of glossy magazines.

"Good," said Freddie. "Then I wouldn't have to be."

Bert Bobbsey threw down his pad and pencil. For the past half hour he'd been going over everything he knew about the case.

"Nothing adds up," he muttered. "We'll have to comb the area for clues all over again. We must have missed something.

"Mom!" he called downstairs. "Where is everyone?"

"Nan's doing an errand for me, and Freddie and Flossie are at the store," she answered.

Not for long, he thought, smiling. They're coming with me to the firehouse.

Freddie finished looking at the new computer magazines.

"Flossie, are you ready to go?"

"Two magazines have stories on Jessica," she said. "I don't have enough money for both. You wouldn't . . ."

"No way," said Freddie.

"I'll just have to decide."

"Don't take all day," he said. "I'll be outside."

On his way out, Freddie got an idea. Maybe the Lost and Found column in the *Lakeport News* would have something on missing puppies.

He bought a copy and took it outside.

A strong wind was blowing. It whipped the newspaper around him. It was hard to keep it open.

Maybe if I sit hunched over, he thought.

By crossing his legs underneath him, Freddie could just squeeze into the wagon. He sat with his back to the wind. Then he started to read the Lost and Found column.

"Doesn't seem to be anything under 'Found,'" he murmured. "It's almost all 'Lost.'

"Look at how many there are. Here's one. 'Fritz, eight-week-old dachshund, disappeared on Monday.' And here's one for a seven-week-old collie. There's Laura's puppy. And a cocker spaniel. And a beagle." He sighed.

"Maybe we'll have to buy a puppy. I wonder how much they cost."

He turned to Pets for Sale. There was quite a long list.

"Hmmm . . . here's one for a collie puppy. . . . Wow! Two hundred and fifty dollars! And look at the price for a beagle—three hundred dollars! I didn't know puppies cost so much."

Freddie continued to read the ads. He was so surprised at the prices, he didn't feel the wind. He didn't hear the traffic. He didn't see anyone come out of the store.

But all of a sudden, he felt something strange. Like someone bumping into him.

He put down the newspaper and the wind blew it out of his hand.

At the same time, the wagon started to roll downhill. But with his legs tucked under him, Freddie couldn't move.

He was stuck in the runaway wagon as it raced down the hill. It bounced along the sidewalk, heading for a team of road workers— right in front of a large, open manhole.

5

Back to the Beginning

The more Nan ran, the thirstier she became. She could feel the perspiration rolling down her forehead. The muscles in her legs began to ache. The thought of a cool, frosty soda started to grow in her mind.

The last quarter of a mile to the grocery store was uphill. She put her head down and turned on the steam.

"Hey! Why don't you watch where you're going?" boomed a voice in front of her.

She looked up and saw Ronald Jameson hurrying by. He didn't recognize her in her running clothes.

Ahead of her, Nan could now see the front of the store. It was just about fifty yards away, up

the street. And there was a red wagon with someone in it, someone with blond hair. The wagon was rolling down the hill—right toward those street workers. And that open manhole!

"FREDDIE!!!" yelled Nan. She took off across the road.

Luckily, there were no cars coming. Nan managed to get to the other side without an accident.

But the wagon was coming at her fast. There was no way she could stop it.

Nan edged to one side and threw a shoulder block. She connected with Freddie, and he was knocked right out of the wagon.

But the wagon kept rolling. It just missed one of the workmen and slammed into his truck.

"You kids!" he shouted, shaking his fist. "You could have been killed. Why don't you watch where you're going?"

Freddie was still lying down on the ground. He hadn't moved yet.

Nan rushed over to him. "Freddie?" she whispered. "Freddie? Are you okay?"

"Yeah," said Freddie. He sat up and rubbed his side. "Where'd you come from? What happened?"

"I just left Laura's house. How come you were rolling down the hill?"

"I don't know," said Freddie. "I think I was pushed."

"Who would do that?" asked Nan.

"Maybe it was an accident," said Freddie.

"You look like you fell off a dump truck," said Nan. "And your jeans—wow!"

"What's wrong with them?" he asked.

"You can't see, but your jeans are split down the back. It must have happened when you fell. We'd better get that fixed right away."

Freddie quickly yanked his T-shirt all the way down to hide the tear.

"Let's get Flossie first. *If* she's made up her mind by now," he said.

Flossie was standing outside the store. Right next to her was Bert.

"What happened to you two? Nan, you look awful. Freddie, you're a mess," said Flossie, all in one breath.

Nan explained how she came across Freddie and what had happened.

"Maybe old man Gower pushed you," said Flossie. "He came in the store right after Freddie left. He looked yucky."

"That doesn't mean anything," said Bert. "Nan, did you find anything at Laura's house?"

Nan told the kids what had happened at the Johnsons'. "I didn't find a clue anywhere," said Nan. "But Mr. Gower was there, too. He drove by right after the boxes fell on me." Nan shuddered as she remembered Mr. Gower's glaring eyes.

"We have to keep looking for clues, then," said Bert. "Has anyone talked to Mom's friend Mrs. Lockhart? Or the Porters?"

"Relax, we will," said Nan. "But Freddie's useless till he gets cleaned up."

"And sewn up," Freddie added. He pulled his T-shirt down more.

"I want to take another look at the fire station," said Bert.

"I'll go with you," said Flossie.

"And I'll start to check out— Hey, where's my newspaper?" said Freddie.

"It must have blown away. I'm sure there's one at home," Nan said.

Just then Mr. Milligan came out of the store.

"Hello," said Nan.

"Hi, kids. How are all the Bobbseys today?" He smiled, but he didn't wait for an answer. In a wink, he was halfway down the street.

"Oh, well," said Nan. "Come on, Freddie."

"Let's go, Flossie," said Bert.

On the way to the firehouse, Flossie told Bert her theories about the missing puppies. The ideas sounded a lot like movies she had just seen on TV.

"Flossie," Bert said, "put all that junk out of

your mind. Concentrate on what we know about the missing puppies."

"I'm not like Freddie," she said. "I don't make lists."

"That's okay, as long as you remember things when you have to," he said.

"I remember what Danny and Ronald said in the candy store," Flossie said. "I'm sure that has something to do with it."

"Candy?"

"No, the license! They said Danny had to get his license," she insisted.

"Maybe it had to do with a dog license for a stolen puppy," Bert said.

"If Danny had a new puppy, everyone would know," said Flossie. "Maybe it was for Ronald."

"Hmmm," said Bert. "We really don't know much about him, do we?"

"I think he's stuck-up," said Flossie.

"Danny said he moved here last week."

"When the puppies started . . . you know," said Flossie. Her voice trembled.

"Tell you what, after we check out the fire station, let's see what we can find out about Ronald," said Bert.

Flossie got an idea.

"We could ask Mom," she said. "Sometimes she interviews new people in town."

Mrs. Bobbsey worked part-time for the *Lakeport News.*

"Or Dad," said Bert. "Maybe the Jamesons bought lumber from him."

The Bobbseys' father owned and operated Lakeport's biggest lumberyard and home improvement center.

"What for?" asked Flossie.

"They'd have to fix up that old house on Maplewood Avenue. No one has lived in it for a long time. Come on, Flossie, I'll race you to the firehouse."

Bert was panting when he caught up to Flossie in front of the firehouse.

"You let me win." She smiled.

"Come on, let's get to work," he said.

For the next several minutes they searched around the outside of the firehouse. They didn't find a single clue.

"Okay, now let's really give the inside a going-over," said Bert.

"Hi, Chief Johnson," said Flossie. She waved to him as he looked up through his office window. "We're going to look back there, where the puppies were. Okay?"

"Go right ahead," he called back to her.

Sparkle came up to them when they approached the back storeroom. Her tail was wagging just a little. Bert and Flossie each gave

Sparkle a pat on the head. Then the dog disappeared alongside one of the two big fire trucks parked inside.

"Sparkle still misses her puppies," said Flossie. "I can tell."

Bert and Flossie stepped into the storeroom.

Bert glanced around. "You, know, this isn't much more than a closet," he said.

"Well," said Flossie, "it was big enough for Sparkle and the seven puppies."

"It's stuffy, too," said Bert. "No windows. Hey, Floss, sounds like there's someone out there. Maybe it's one of the fire fighters. Let's go ask if any of them saw anything—you know, when . . ."

Just as they turned to leave the little room, the door slammed.

"Dumb wind," said Bert.

He turned the doorknob. It didn't move.

He pushed against the door. It was closed tight.

"What's the matter?" asked Flossie.

"The door's locked," Bert said angrily.

"Knock on it. Someone will hear," she said, a touch of fear in her voice.

They started to bang on the door.

Suddenly a loud clanging began outside. A siren wailed high above their heads.

"It's the fire alarm," said Bert.

They could hear the engines start up as the fire trucks began to roll.

The bell rang, the siren wailed. The trucks revved their engines and drove away.

The firehouse was deserted as the fire fighters went racing off.

No one could hear Bert and Flossie.

They were trapped.

6

A Key Decision

"There, you're all fixed," said Nan. "It doesn't look that great, but those jeans are almost worn out anyhow."

"Just the way I like them," said Freddie. He strutted back and forth.

"Now that's taken care of," said Nan, "I want to check on something. By myself."

"What can I do?" Freddie asked eagerly.

"Take a break—eat an apple or something," said Nan. And she marched off.

Freddie looked at the fruit bowl on the table. It made him think of something he couldn't remember. What was it?

Maybe he ought to help Bert and Flossie. He took an apple and headed for the firehouse.

Nan, meanwhile, had gone into the Bobbseys' garage. They'd put Freddie's wagon away before they dealt with his torn jeans.

I didn't get a real good look at this before, she thought. Let me just see, now . . .

Nan picked up the rope tied to the wagon's handle.

"Just as I suspected," she murmured. "It's been cut. Hmm . . . Dad says a leopard can't change its spots. But maybe a person can change."

Nan wheeled her bike out of the garage.

"It's time I did some more investigating," she said. "At Mr. Gower's place."

As he headed for the firehouse, Freddie thought about the rope, too.

He knew he'd tied that rope really tight. So it must have been cut. Who could have done that?

The big front doors of the firehouse were wide open, but there were no fire trucks inside. And no fire fighters to be seen.

Freddie figured they must be answering an alarm. "Wish I could have been here to see them go," he murmured.

Freddie stood in the center of the large room. It's awfully quiet when no one's around, he thought.

Suddenly he heard a sound. It was coming from Sparkle's room.

As he got closer to the back room Freddie could hear muffled noises.

"Maybe the puppies are back," he cried as he rushed toward the door.

Wait a minute, those were human voices!

Freddie pressed his ear against the door and heard: "Help! Let us out of here!"

It was Bert.

"It's hot. I can't breathe."

That was Flossie.

"Hey, it's me," shouted Freddie. He pulled on the door. It was locked tight and wouldn't budge.

"Get someone to let us out," called Bert through the door.

"There's no one here," answered Freddie, looking around.

"Quick, see if you can find a key," said Bert.

Freddie made a fast search. The area was spotless. Everything was in order. And there was no key to be found.

"I can't find it!" he shouted through the door.

"You'll have to pick the lock," said Bert.

"Oh, sure," said Freddie.

"Listen, I know how to do it. Find something thin and hard, like a credit card," said Bert.

On a nearby table Freddie saw a small calendar given out by the Lakeport Savings Bank.

"Is a wallet-size bank calendar any good?" he asked.

"Great," said Bert. "It's plastic-coated, so it should work. Now slide it in between the door and the frame, just below the lock."

"Okay," said Freddie, after a moment. "I did, but nothing happened."

"Push it up and wiggle it a little."

Nothing.

"Try pushing it right where the thingy goes in the whatsit. You know, where the lock goes into the hole."

That did it. The lock sprung open.

Bert and Flossie practically fell out of the tiny room.

Suddenly the firehouse was filled with the noise of engines. The big red fire trucks came rolling back from the fire.

Chief Johnson jumped out from behind the driver's seat.

"False alarm," he grumbled. Then he noticed the Bobbseys. "What are you kids doing here?"

Bert told him what happened.

"Never a dull minute around this place," said the chief. "First the puppies disappear, then that caterer, Mulligan . . ."

"Do you mean Mr. Milligan?" asked Freddie.

"Right. Milligan," said Chief Johnson. "He came back to give me prices for the Firemen's

Ball. They were a lot higher than when he was here earlier."

"When was that?" asked Freddie. "He was at our house yesterday morning."

"Oh, around noontime," said the chief. "Right around the time that kid I saw you talking to was looking at the pups."

"You mean the dark-haired guy? Outside the firehouse?" asked Bert.

"No, the tall, skinny one. I haven't seen him around. Must be new in town. I know the other one, the Rugg boy."

"Do you remember anything else about when the puppies disappeared?" asked Bert.

"Look, young man," said the chief, "I told you and your sister everything I know. Now, don't start bothering me."

"Sorry, Chief," said Bert. He turned to Freddie. "Let's make tracks."

Nan pedaled across town as quickly as she could. She had to check out her hunch.

The neat, trim lawns and freshly cut hedges began to disappear as she rode along. Here, at the far side of town, the houses were not kept up as well. Paint had peeled, and roofs were missing shingles. Trash barrels sat rusting on curbs. Litter collected in the gutters.

"I know it's around here somewhere," she murmured.

There it was: Gower. The mailbox sat tilted to one side on a bent fence post.

"Now, let's just see if Old Man Gower has taken to grabbing puppies," Nan said to herself.

She decided to try her trusty old collecting-for-charity routine. She went up to the front door.

There was no doorbell and no brass knocker. Nan rapped on the heavy door with her knuckles.

No answer.

She knocked again.

Still no answer.

Well, if no one's home, I might as well take a look for myself, she thought.

Nan strolled casually to the back of the house. There was a long, low shack that edged right up to the back porch. High up on top was a row of dirty, screened windows. Even standing on tiptoe, she couldn't see inside. But she could hear dogs yapping and barking.

Could that be where Mr. Gower was hiding the puppies?

She went around to the side, where she found a wooden door with a rusty latch.

"All I need is a peek inside," she murmured.

Nan unhitched the latch and pressed the door forward.

BRRINNNGGGGG!

WHEEE-EW! WHEEE-EW!
HONK! HONK! HONK!
Bells, whistles, and sirens sounded, telling the whole neighborhood there was a burglar. And that burglar was Nan Bobbsey.

7

Two for the Road

The rusty old pickup truck stopped in front of the Bobbsey house.

Nan Bobbsey climbed out the passenger side. She went around back and hauled down her bicycle.

"Thank you for the lift, Mr. Gower," Nan said quietly. Then she added, "And I'm sorry for . . . well, you know."

"I do," he said angrily. "Just don't jump to conclusions in the future."

He pulled away from the curb and drove off.

As Nan came in the house, Bert stopped her. "What was all that about?" he asked.

"Oh, just a little mistake . . . something dumb," she mumbled.

"Did it have anything to do with the puppies?" he asked.

"Okay, I might as well tell you," Nan said with a sigh.

She described her visit to the Gower house and her surprise out back.

"A lot of the neighborhood kids bother him," Nan explained. "And they try to do mean things to the stray dogs he finds. So Mr. Gower set up this booby trap in his shed. When the siren and the bells and everything went off, he came running from around the corner."

"But did you see any sign of the puppies?" asked Bert.

"Nothing," she said sadly. "I even came right out and asked him. It's like we've always heard—he just picks up strays."

"Why'd you go there, anyhow?" asked Bert.

"Well, I did see him around Laura's house," Nan said. "And I found this dog food coupon near her garage. I kept thinking that maybe someone who bought a lot of dog food might . . . you know."

"Pretty farfetched, if you ask me," said Bert, frowning.

"Well, I didn't ask you," snapped Nan. "Anyway, I told Mr. Gower that, too. He laughed and said he only buys 'no-frills' dog food because it's the cheapest. He doesn't even bother with coupons."

"Come on," said Bert. "Let's get something to drink. We've got a lot to go over."

Later that afternoon, the four Bobbseys gathered in Nan's room.

"So I made a mistake with Mr. Gower, but there's something else bothering me. And I don't mean just the missing puppies," Nan said, pacing back and forth.

"What do you mean?" asked Freddie, looking up from the newspaper he was reading.

"Someone's trying to scare us away from finding those puppies," she said. "First it was Freddie's wagon. The rope was definitely cut. Then the storeroom door in the firehouse. The wind didn't blow it shut."

"And what about those boxes falling on you at Laura's?" said Flossie.

"You know something?" said Freddie. "Every time something happens, I think about that Ronald Jameson. Didn't you see him just before you ran after my wagon, Nan?"

"That's right," she said, climbing onto the bed.

"He was at the firehouse around the time the puppies disappeared, too," Bert said.

"He could have followed you to Laura's

house," said Freddie. He was getting excited.

"And then beat me back to the store to cut you loose?" she said. "Not on foot. And I'm sure he isn't old enough to drive."

"Maybe that's why they need a license," suggested Flossie. "Or maybe Danny's driving his father's car without a license?"

"Wait a minute," said Nan. "They say they've teamed up to solve the crime. How about this—maybe they got together to commit the crime, too."

Bert was puzzled.

"I don't get it," he said.

"You know how much Danny hates it that we've solved a few crimes. Well, maybe he decided that he could solve the one crime that he knows more about than anyone else—the one *he* committed," she explained.

"And he got that stuck-up Ronald to help him," added Flossie.

"Sounds dumb to me," said Freddie.

"It's not much to go on," said Nan, "but it's all we have for now."

"I agree," said Bert. "Here's the plan—Nan and I will go over to see Danny and Ronald. We'll find out where they were when the puppies disappeared. *And* when all these other things happened."

"What about us?" asked Flossie.

"You two split up," Bert suggested. "One of

you visit Mrs. Porter. The other take the Lockhart house. They're both nearby. Find out anything you can about the day the puppies disappeared."

"Good idea, Bert," said Nan. "Come on,
let's get on our bikes."

No sooner had they left than Mr. Milligan
pulled up in his van. He had a load of party
supplies to deliver.

Mrs. Bobbsey asked Freddie and Flossie to
help him unload.

"Careful you don't spill anything. Mrs. Milligan packed things exactly as we need them.
She does the packing, I do the driving," he
said. He went inside the house with a tall car-
ton.

"Mrs. Milligan is very fussy," said Flossie. "I
could tell. Did you see the printing on those
menus? Very fancy-looking."

"Be careful," called Mr. Milligan from the
doorway. "Watch that box, please. It has all the
doilies for the hors d'oeuvres."

"The what for the what?" said Freddie.

"Hors d'oeuvres is a fancy word for snacks,"
Mr. Milligan said with a smile.

"And you put doilies underneath things," explained Flossie.

"Remember," Mr. Milligan called out, again.
"Don't drop—"

Just then there was a loud crash.

Mr. Milligan had just dropped a coffee urn.

"Oh, no, I can't believe I did that," said Mr. Milligan in the distance.

Freddie pressed his lips together to keep from giggling.

But Flossie just burst out laughing.

Nan and Bert pedaled their bikes down the long road that led to Danny's house.

"Might as well try him first," said Bert.

"Right," Nan agreed. "We don't have a lot to go on."

"I know. But we can't sit around just waiting for clues to fall in our lap. We have to find those puppies soon," he said firmly.

"It wouldn't surprise me if that Ronald kid put Danny up to it," said Nan. "He looks—and sounds—like a *real* troublemaker. Just what Danny needs!"

They came to the intersection where Maplewood Avenue branched off the main road.

"You know what?" said Bert. "Why don't we tackle Ronald first?"

"Why not?" Nan shrugged her shoulders. "We're right here."

The street curved in a long arch, lined with maple trees. Ronald's house was the fourth one down on the right.

As Bert and Nan came closer, they could see something happening in front of his house.

There was someone kneeling. Someone else was lying on the ground, right near the curb.

"That guy is probably doing some warm-up exercises," Nan said.

"It's Ronald," said Bert as they got closer. "Look, he's trying to help the person lying on the ground."

"Hey! That person has been injured."

Nan gasped. "It's Danny Rugg!"

8

Instant Recovery

Flossie reached for a cookie.

"Yes, it's really awfully sad," she said. "How long did you have the puppy before it . . . disappeared?"

"We got it a few weeks before our anniversary," said Mrs. Porter. "We hadn't even decided to give the party, but it was such fun. And then the puppy disappeared." She shook her head sadly.

"And there were no clues? Nothing broken? Nothing missing?" asked Flossie.

"Nothing." Mrs. Porter sighed. "The police said it looked like an 'inside job.' How silly! Who would want to steal our new puppy? And everyone at the party was our friend."

"Yes, it really is sad," said Flossie. "May I have another cookie?"

* * *

Freddie walked behind Mr. Lockhart as he trimmed the hedge.

Snip! Snip! Branches and twigs kept falling.

"I told Louise something would happen. Big party like that. Bound to be some kind of trouble," said Mr. Lockhart.

"What do you mean . . . 'trouble'?" asked Freddie. Maybe there was a clue here.

"You know, break a lamp, knock over the punch bowl," said Mr. Lockhart. "Never thought the party would go smoothly. And then, the trouble."

"You mean the puppy?" asked Freddie.

"Right," said Mr. Lockhart. "Ruined the whole evening. Not to mention the cost."

"Of the party?"

"And the puppy," said Mr. Lockhart. "Pedigreed cocker spaniels don't come cheap, you know."

"I do know," Freddie said. "And you don't know how it happened? Or why?"

"Not a clue," said Mr. Lockhart.

Snip! Snip! Snip!

Nan stared at the body lying on the pavement.

"What happened?" she asked. She looked down but couldn't see Danny's face. It was turned toward the ground.

"Hit and run," said Ronald. "Pretty bad. But luckily I got the license number."

"Shouldn't you call an ambulance?" asked Nan.

"I already called the police," said Ronald. "They'll take care of things when they get here."

Bert came around the other side. He stared at Danny.

"Sure is too bad he's unconscious—or worse," said Bert casually. "I guess he'll never know about the new summer softball coach. Especially since— Well, never mind."

Danny's body jerked sharply. He lifted his head.

"What do you mean, 'the new coach'?" he demanded. "What happened to Coach Shapiro?"

"Danny! You're not unconscious!" Nan said.

"What are you pulling, Bert Bobbsey?" shouted Danny. He jumped up. "If you're trying to get the new coach to take me off the roster, I'll fix you."

"You're not hurt, either!" Bert said angrily. "You were just faking. What's the idea? Looking for clues in the road?"

"Some detective." Nan laughed.

"Oh, yeah?" sneered Danny. "I don't care what you think. What's this about a new coach?"

"There isn't any," said Bert. "I thought you were faking. So I said that to see if you'd bite."

"And you did," Nan said happily.

"Big deal," snapped Ronald. "Who cares? We already have the cops working for us."

"Sure, the whole police force is out looking for lost puppies," said Bert.

Ronald snickered. "They may not know it, but they are doing a job for us."

"What do you mean?" asked Nan.

"Go ahead, Ronald," said Danny. "Tell them."

"You Bobbseys might as well admit we've outsmarted you," Ronald said smugly.

"Ronald saw the thieves," said Danny.

"He did?" said Nan. "I don't believe it."

"Well, he saw the van they were driving," said Danny. "The day they took the puppies from the firehouse. Ronald was across the street at the candy store."

"Right after he checked out the puppies himself?" asked Bert.

"Uh-huh," said Danny. "He saw this really wild van right in front of the firehouse. Painted with all kinds of crazy stuff. Couldn't miss the license plate—B-U-Z-Z-B."

"Now all we need to know is who owns that van. Then we'll have the thieves in our pocket," said Ronald.

"We called the cops and told them it was that

van that hit me. Knocked me right over,"
Danny said proudly. "They'll pick up the
crooks."

"Thanks to *our* brilliant detective work,"
Ronald said. He smiled nastily.

"I can't believe you guys," said Bert, shaking
his head. "You have to be out of your minds. If
you think—"

The wail of a siren interrupted him. A black
and white police car, with a flashing red and
blue light on top, came speeding down the
road. It stopped in front of the Jameson house.

Sergeant Molly Franklin got out of the car
and walked over to Danny. He was sitting on
the curb now.

"Well, look who's here, half the Bobbsey
Detective Agency. And how are Bert and Nan
today?" she asked.

"Fine, Sergeant Franklin," said Nan. She was
pleased to see a friendly face.

"Glad to hear it. Are you the one who got
hit?" she asked, looking down at Danny.

"Well," he mumbled, "it just sort of grazed
me."

"Right." She looked at Ronald. "And you're
the one who got the number? Who called it in?"

"Just doing my duty, miss," Ronald said. He
gave her an innocent smile.

"It's *Officer*. Or *Sergeant*. And don't forget
it," she said. "Now, perhaps you boys can an-

swer a few simple questions. About the truck you saw . . ."

"It was a van," said Ronald.

"The one with the license plate B-U-Z-Z-B," she said.

Nan scratched her head.

"That sounds like that rock-'n'-roll group that played at the high school prom last year, The Buzzbees," she said.

"Are they back in town?" asked Bert.

"They were the other day," said Sergeant Franklin. "They stopped at the fire station to play a cassette for Chief Johnson."

"Wow," said Bert. "I never figured him for a rock fan."

"He isn't," said Sergeant Franklin. "They were trying to get a job playing for the Firemen's Ball. The chief was polite, but no dice."

"So they stole all his puppies?" Ronald suggested.

"Of course not," said Sergeant Franklin. "He saw them off—for Canada. They left a number in case he changed his mind. We called. The van's parked in their hotel garage right now."

"Whoops!" said Nan, smiling.

Sergeant Franklin turned to Danny.

"So perhaps you could tell me how it is that it just missed running you down. And you, of course," she added, pointing to Ronald, "you saw the number."

Bert looked at Nan. They both knew it was time for them to leave quietly. They got on their bikes and started pedaling down the street.

"I wonder what'll happen to Ronald and Danny now," called Nan.

"Sergeant Franklin will probably let them off easy—*this* time," Bert said with a laugh.

Back in the Bobbsey kitchen, Bert and Nan told Freddie and Flossie what had happened. They listened as the younger twins described their visits to the Porter and Lockhart houses.

"At least we know that Danny and Ronald don't know anything we don't know," said Freddie.

"But what *do* we know?" Nan said.

"It's a real mystery," said Bert, frowning. "No sign of anything broken. Not even the locks on the doors."

"Do you think the thief has a bunch of keys?" said Flossie. "Is that how he gets the puppies?"

"Why do you think it's a *he*?" asked Nan. "It could just as easily be a *she*."

"Or a whole gang," Freddie put in.

"I'm still not convinced that Ronald and Danny aren't part of it," said Bert. "We never did get to ask them any questions."

The twins' discussion was interrupted by a loud thump in front of the house.

"What was that?" said Nan, jumping up.

The four Bobbseys went to the front door. They opened it cautiously.

Lying on the porch was a small package.

They unwrapped it and saw a brick-size chunk of Styrofoam, in two pieces.

"Open it up," said Freddie.

"Let's see what's inside," said Flossie, squirming with curiosity.

Bert separated the two pieces of Styrofoam.

"Look," said Freddie. "It's a tape."

"Who wants to listen to music now?" said Flossie, yawning.

"Maybe we'd better," said Nan. "Flossie, come on, get your portable tape player."

Flossie brought the bright yellow tape deck into the kitchen. Bert put on the tape.

First there were a few barks. Next came a muffled voice, like someone talking through a tube. They could just make out what it said.

"Stop trying to find the puppies. Or there's going to be trouble. Something terrible could happen. Not to you . . . but definitely . . . to the puppies."

9

Classified Information

The morning of the big party started out cloudy. There was electricity in the air and the possibility of a thunderstorm.

"Your mother's really excited about this party," said Mr. Bobbsey before he left for work. "I know you kids will help in any way you can. And after it's all over, well, maybe we can talk about getting you a little treat."

"A puppy?" asked Flossie. "We're going to find ours." Tears began to well up in her eyes.

"We'll see," said Mr. Bobbsey quietly. He gently stroked Flossie's hair. Then he got into his car and drove off.

The four Bobbsey twins moved to the back porch, to be out of the way. Two days had

d since they had found the threatening
There had been no new developments and
new clues.

I just hope the puppies are being fed prop-
y," said Flossie.

"You mean, are they getting any puppy
reats?" said Freddie, teasing her.

Nan held her hands up in protest.

"Come on," she said. "We've got a real decision to make."

"Like when to tell Mom and Dad about the
tape," Bert said firmly. "Remember, we agreed
to hold off until sometime after the party. I
mean, what can they do?"

"They can be really angry if anything happens," said Freddie. "And for punishment, no
TV, no burgers—"

"Stop!" said Flossie. She put her hands to her
ears. "I don't want to hear any more bad
things."

A crunch of gravel told them a car had ar-
rived in the driveway.

"It's Mr. Milligan again," announced Freddie. "Probably with another load of party
things. More streamers to put up and doilies to
put down. I'm beginning to hate parties."

Mr. Milligan came in the back door.

"No puppy yet?" he asked. "I thought you
might have gotten another one."

"We're not going to," said Freddie. "We're going to find *our* puppy. And we're going to find all the others, too."

He ran angrily from the room.

Mrs. Bobbsey almost collided with him as she entered the kitchen.

"You'll have to forgive Freddie," she said, apologizing. "He feels very, very bad about the lost puppies."

"They're not lost," Flossie insisted. "They're stolen. And I hate whoever stole them."

She, too, stormed out of the room.

"Such emotional children," said Mr. Milligan. "Well, let's get down to businss. There are some boxes out there that need to come in."

"Come on, Nan," said Bert. "We'll have to do it. I can see Freddie out there on his bike already."

Freddie wasn't going far. He locked the handlebars in place and pedaled away in a large circle. That was his favorite way of thinking things out.

There was something he couldn't quite remember. Something that might be a piece of the puzzle. If he could just remember what it was . . .

He thought all the way back to the day Bert came home without the puppy.

What was the first thing he had done on his

own? The newspaper! That was it. He had been reading about the other lost puppies. And the new ones for sale. But he had lost the paper when he went spinning down the street.

He wanted another look at those ads.

He found a copy of the *Lakeport News* inside the house and took it to his room.

Flossie heard him across the hall reading out loud.

" 'Cocker spaniel puppy for sale—two hundred and fifty dollars.' Wow! That's a lot of money."

Bert and Nan came into his room.

"Now that we've done all the work," said Bert, tucking in his shirt, "what are you up to?"

"I've been looking at the paper. It sure costs a lot to buy a puppy," Freddie said.

"Only if it has a pedigree," said Nan.

"What's that?" asked Flossie, as she entered the room.

"It's like a birth certificate, with grandparents and great-grandparents, and great-great-grandparents—as far back as they can go," said Nan.

"Does every puppy have one?" asked Flossie. She flopped on Freddie's bed.

"No," said Bert. "Only the really fancy ones. That's what makes them cost so much."

"Do Sparkle's puppies have pe-di-grees?" asked Flossie, saying the new word slowly.

"I guess so," said Nan. "They're supposed to be purebred dalmatians."

Bert was scanning the list of lost puppies.

"Beagle . . . cocker spaniel . . . Airedale. That makes three," said Bert. "If you add on the seven dalmatian puppies, that's ten stolen puppies."

"Isn't that strange?" said Nan. "We know the people they were stolen from."

"Mmmmm," said Flossie. "And some of them are coming to Mom's party tonight."

"Most of them had their own parties already," said Freddie.

"And that's when their puppies disappeared!" said Nan.

"All of them except our puppy," said Flossie.

"But there was going to be a party—the Firemen's Ball. Chief Johnson said something about it the same day Sparkle's puppies were stolen," said Nan.

"That's when Mr. and Mrs. Milligan dropped off some menus at our house," Bert said.

"And I found one of their blue lacy things," said Freddie.

"A doily?" said Flossie.

"I found it near the back room in the firehouse. I thought it was just a piece of scrap paper."

"Puppies disappeared from every place where

the Milligans were catering a party," said Nan, getting excited.

"Do you think . . . ?" asked Bert.

"How'd they do it?" asked Freddie.

"And why?" asked Flossie. "Especially our puppy."

"I bet they thought it was one of those fancy ones, worth a lot of money," said Freddie.

"We don't know that yet," said Bert.

"There are a lot of questions that still need answering," Nan said calmly.

The twins agreed not to jump to conclusions. Nan still smarted from her visit to Mr. Gower. They would act as though they still knew nothing—until after the party. But they would watch the Milligans very carefully.

That evening, the weather cleared. A lovely sunset cast its glow on the Bobbsey house as the party began.

Just as they expected, the twins were asked to help out. They passed plates with little sandwiches. They refilled the ice bucket. They ran for towels when people spilled things.

When the party was in full swing, Flossie took Freddie aside.

"I'm sure it's the Milligans. They just look guilty to me," she whispered.

"I know," he whispered back.

"Have some of those little meatballs," Mrs.

Bobbsey said to the two of them. "They're Mrs. Milligan's specialty."

She looked past them and saw someone in the doorway.

"Oh, Alice, I'm glad you could make it," Mrs. Bobbsey said. Off she went across the room.

"I can't stand to think of the puppies all by themselves," Flossie said.

"Think they are?" asked Freddie. "Where?"

"One guess. At the Milligans' shop, probably."

"Here's an oldie but goodie," said Mr. Bobbsey, changing the tape on the stereo. "This ought to set some toes tapping."

"No one would miss us," said Freddie.

"You must try these delicious chicken wings," said Mrs. Bobbsey to Mrs. Lockhart. "Oh, I forgot—you already know what Mrs. Milligan can do."

Freddie and Flossie edged their way out of the living room. In a few minutes they were on their bikes.

It didn't take them long to ride to the Milligans' shop.

When they got there, the shop was dark. The doors were locked, too. But there was a small window in the back where the kitchen was. It was open just a crack.

They pushed hard, and it slid up.

Freddie hoisted Flossie up. She climbed through the window. Freddie climbed in after her.

They looked around the shop but found nothing.

"Good thing we brought this flashlight," Freddie whispered.

"What about that door over there?" Flossie whispered back.

"Probably just another closet," Freddie said, but he pulled it open anyhow. He shone the flashlight into the doorway. A flight of stairs led down to the cellar.

Flossie found a light switch and turned it on. Then she and Freddie went down the steps. The first thing they found in the cellar was a small printing press. A large, open can of ink was on the floor, right next to it.

At the back of the room, filling up almost half the cellar, were cages, all piled up.

The cages were filled with puppies!

They whined and barked and scampered when Flossie went over to them.

"Oh, Freddie," cried Flossie, "it's the puppies! Let's take them all home with us!"

"They're not going anywhere," came a loud voice from the top of the stairs. "And neither are you."

10

Losers Weepers

Meanwhile, the party at the Bobbsey house was in full swing.

"Seems to me that we're doing all the work," said Nan.

"What did you say?" Bert asked. "I can hardly hear you with that music on. I didn't know that music from the old days could be so loud."

"Where are Freddie and Flossie?" she shouted at him.

Mrs. Bobbsey came up to them.

"Would one of you check in the kitchen and see if there are any more chicken wings?" she asked. "I just want to have a dance with your father."

Nan shook her head and laughed. "Okay, Mom."

She headed for the kitchen.

"And Bert," called Mrs. Bobbsey from the dance floor, "would you get a towel?"

He followed Nan into the kitchen.

"Looks like Flossie and Freddie cut out," said Bert.

"You think they found out something?" asked Nan.

"If they did, they might have decided to check it out themselves," he said.

"That could be dangerous," she said.

Bert looked around.

"Especially since I don't see the Milligans anywhere," he said.

"You're right!" said Nan, staring at the empty kitchen. "And they sure weren't out there," she added, pointing to the party.

Bert opened the closet near the back door.

"Their coats are gone!" he said.

"We'd better not break up the party," Nan said. "But I think we ought to call Sergeant Franklin and tell her what's going on. It's time. Flossie and Freddie could be in real trouble."

"Go ahead," said Bert. "Make that call."

Inside the shop, Mr. Milligan stood at the top of the stairs.

"You rotten kids!" he shouted. "You wouldn't listen, would you?"

"*You* made that tape," gasped Flossie.

"So you figured it out, did you? Well, it's too late now," Mr. Milligan said as he came down the stairs. "We had a nice thing going here. Then you started butting in."

He came forward, reaching for Flossie. But Freddie was closer and blocked the way. He quickly knocked over the can of ink.

"Get out of the—" Suddenly Mr. Milligan slipped on the ink and landed on his side.

Flossie ran to the back of the cellar and opened the cages.

"Shoo, shoo, out you go," she called. "At least you'll be free now."

More than ten puppies scampered around the room. They ran through the spilled ink, across Mr. Milligan, and up the stairs into the shop.

"I'll get you!" yelled Mr. Milligan, slipping and sliding.

Freddie and Flossie raced around him and up the stairs.

There, at the top, stood Mrs. Milligan, trying to grab the runaway puppies.

"We told you to mind your own business," she shouted. "We had a nice operation going! Even printed our own phony pedigrees for these dumb mutts.

"Work a party and grab a puppy. Then Albert here got greedy. Had to go for all seven at the firehouse in one move. He couldn't wait for your parents' party for just one. Well, we can

still make a nice piece of money on them.

"But first . . ." She came running toward the twins. Both children reached the top of the stairs, dodged her, and ran into the kitchen. Flossie huddled behind Freddie.

The puppies were all over the place, running wild. They knocked over boxes filled with paper cups, confetti, and napkins. They got into the bins of sugar and flour.

Mr. Milligan limped up the stairs.

"Quick, get the front door," he shouted to Mrs. Milligan. She dashed forward and blocked that escape. He stood in the back of the shop. There was no way around him.

"Now, you little monsters," said Mrs. Milligan, "let's see you try to get out of this. You've been a real pain, and it's time—"

Thump! Thump! Thump!

There was a pounding on the front door behind Mrs. Milligan.

Rap! Rap! Rap!

The sound of someone tapping on the back window came from behind Mr. Milligan.

"It might be the police!" cried Mrs. Milligan. "Turn off the lights. We'll try to escape through the loading dock."

They hurried toward a door in the side wall. Suddenly the door was yanked open.

A flashing red and blue light shone on the startled faces of Mr. and Mrs. Milligan.

"Planning to go somewhere?" said the bright voice of Sergeant Franklin. "I think you'll be comfortable with the little ride we've arranged. Straight to the police station."

"Am I ever glad to see you, Sergeant Molly," said Flossie.

Freddie found the light switch and turned it on. The puppies were still bouncing about the shop.

"Look, they're all there," came a voice from the window.

"Bert!" called Freddie. "Come on in."

He opened the front door. Bert and Nan rushed inside.

Nan laughed when she saw Flossie.

"Just look at you," Nan said. "Flossie, you're a real mess."

"I don't care," said Flossie. She was holding a shaggy, smudged bundle in her arms. "It was worth it."

"Wait a minute," said Bert. He stared at the puppy in Flossie's arms. "That's not a dalmatian."

"It looks like a sheepdog." Nan leaned over and scratched the puppy behind one ear.

"I remember the kinds of dogs that were on that Lost and Found list," Freddie said with excitement. "It didn't say anything about a sheepdog."

"It might be a stray," said Sergeant Franklin.

"I'll check it out later. Right now let's round up the *rest* of the puppies and see that they all get back to their owners."

But the Bobbseys weren't listening to Sergeant Franklin. They were too busy taking turns cuddling the shaggy puppy.

"I hope it is a stray." The sergeant smiled. "Because it looks like this puppy has found itself a new home."

When the police van pulled up in front of the Bobbsey house, the party was still in full swing.

Mrs. Bobbsey came to the front door.

"Have the neighbors complained?" she asked. Then she saw the strange group that stepped out of the back of the van—Bert and Nan, a bedraggled Freddie and Flossie, four bicycles, and a wiggling ball of fur in Flossie's arms. She was covered with inky paw prints.

"Maybe you'd all better come in through the kitchen," said Mrs. Bobbsey. "Let me get your father."

Inside the kitchen, the kids explained how they had begun to suspect the Milligans when they read the list of missing puppies.

"And the ones for sale, too," added Bert.

"Then we remembered Mr. Milligan coming out of the store after Freddie's wagon was cut loose," said Nan.

"Right after he got through dumping those boxes on you at Laura's house," said Freddie.

"Right," agreed Nan. "He probably came by to take them to the dump."

"Yes," said Mrs. Bobbsey. "That's part of their service."

"Probably gives them a chance to double-check, see if they've left any clues," said Nan.

"Well, they missed one clue," Freddie said. "The blue doily on the floor of the fire-house."

"Mr. Milligan must have been keeping an eye on Flossie and me. He saw us go to the fire-house," said Bert. "Then he tried to scare us by locking Flossie and me in that storeroom."

"I bet he told Mrs. Milligan to call in a false alarm," said Freddie.

"Why did you decide to go to their shop in the middle of the party?" asked Mrs. Bobbsey.

"We agreed to watch them," said Freddie. "And we saw how they never looked at Mrs. Lockhart, or Mrs. Porter."

"They couldn't face the people they stole puppies from," said Flossie.

"And we figured we might be able to get the puppies while they were busy here," added Freddie.

"Well, it's a good thing someone had enough sense to call the police," said Mr. Bobbsey.

"Right," Nan said proudly. "But we had to see for ourselves what was going on."

"So we headed over on our bikes, too," Bert explained.

"They certainly had a lot of people fooled." Mrs. Bobbsey sighed. "I couldn't figure out how they catered parties so cheaply."

"Just their way of getting a foot in the door," said Mr. Bobbsey.

"And a puppy out," said Nan.

"They must have heard that we were getting a puppy," said Bert. "That's why they offered to do your party."

"But when they got here and found out where the puppy was coming from, Mr. Milligan decided to go for all of them," said Nan.

"Too bad Ronald didn't see him instead of the Buzzbees," said Freddie.

"Hey, whatever happened to Ronald and Danny, anyhow?" asked Flossie.

Nan smiled. "Sergeant Franklin told me they're being punished for calling in a false report. But that's all."

"Are they going to jail?" asked Freddie.

"No," said Nan. "They have to work down at the police station for the next two weeks—cleaning up the police dog kennels."

"Speaking of dogs," said Mr. Bobbsey.

"You're going to let us keep the puppy, aren't you?" asked Freddie.

"Please," Nan begged.

Before Mr. and Mrs. Bobbsey could say anything, the telephone rang.

"I'll get it," Bert said, grabbing up the receiver. "Hello?" Slowly a grin spread over his face. "There isn't? . . . Are you sure? . . . Well, thanks for calling." Bert hung up the phone.

"Guess what?" he said. "That was Sergeant Franklin. She says the police have no report of a missing sheepdog—so the puppy is ours. Isn't it, Mom? Dad?"

Mr. and Mrs. Bobbsey looked at each other.

"How could we say no now?" Mr. Bobbsey said with a smile.

"I think we should call him Shag," said Mrs. Bobbsey.

"That's no name for a dog," said Mr. Bobbsey. "How about Sport?"

"Too common," she said. "What about . . ."

The four Bobbsey twins quietly left the kitchen and went upstairs.

When they reached the landing, Flossie broke their silence.

"Tomorrow morning we can tell them. His name is Chief."